SLIP

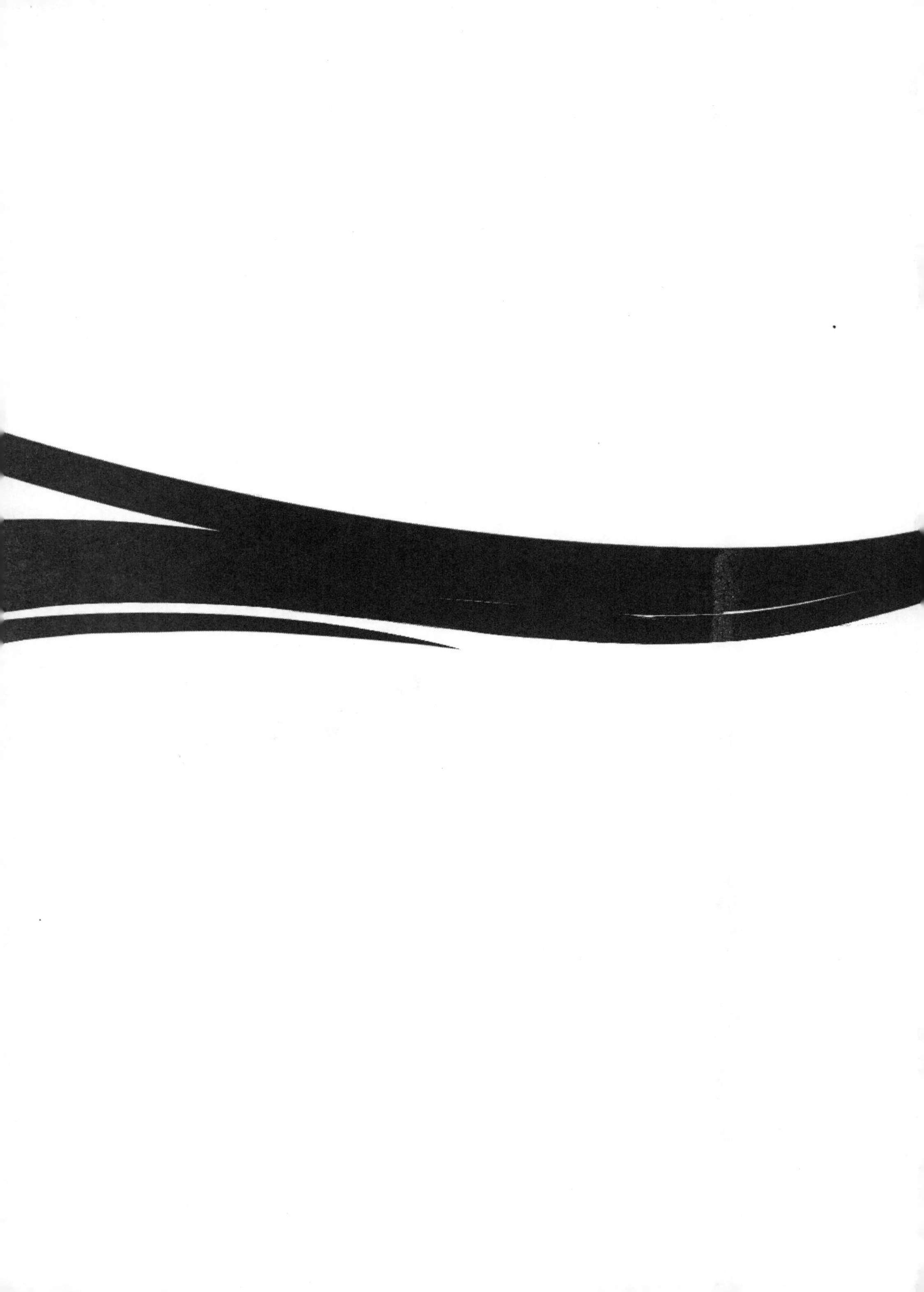

SLIP

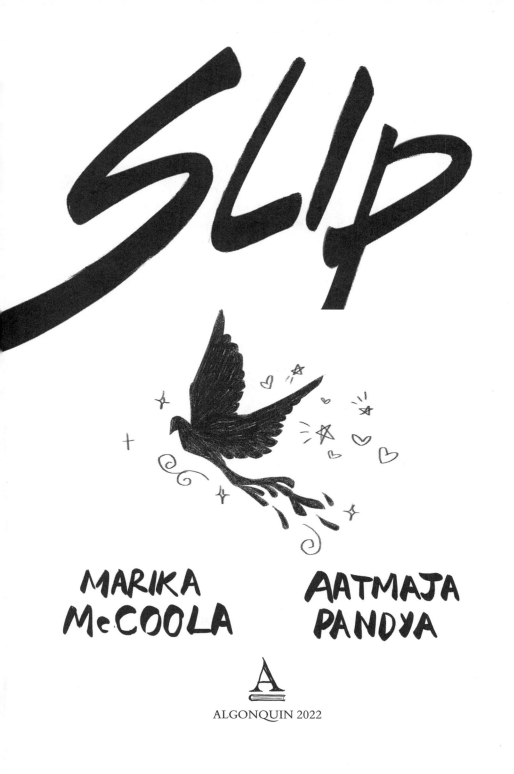

MARIKA McCOOLA

AATMAJA PANDYA

ALGONQUIN 2022

Published by Algonquin Young Readers
an imprint of Algonquin Books of Chapel Hill
Post Office Box 2225
Chapel Hill, North Carolina 27515-2225

a division of Workman Publishing
225 Varick Street
New York, New York 10014

Printed in the United States of America
Design by Neil Swaab

LIBRARY OF CONGRESS CATALOGING-IN-PUBLICATION DATA

Names: McCoola, Marika, author. | Pandya, Aatmaja, illustrator.
Title: Slip / Marika McCoola, Aatmaja Pandya.
Description: First edition. | Chapel Hill, North Carolina : Algonquin Young Readers, 2022. |
Audience: Ages 14 and up | Audience: Grades 10–12 |
Summary: "A young pottery student finds her artistic voice and first love at an art camp, while also coping with feelings of guilt and worry about her best friend, who recently attempted suicide"—Provided by publisher.
Identifiers: LCCN 2021062830 | ISBN 9781616207892 (trade paperback) |
ISBN 9781643752495 (hardcover) | ISBN 9781643752907 (ebook)
Subjects: CYAC: Artists—Fiction. | Camp—Fiction. | Love—Fiction. | Friendship—Fiction. |
LCGFT: Coming-of-age comics. | Graphic novels.
Classification: LCC PZ7.7.M417 Sli 2022 | DDC 741.5/973—dc23/eng/20220131
LC record available at https://lccn.loc.gov/2021062830

ISBN 978-1-61620-789-2 (PB)
ISBN 978-1-64375-249-5 (HC)

10 9 8 7 6 5 4 3 2 1
First Edition

To the people from prior chapters

—M. M.

For Mota Masi, the artist, and Ba,
who loved beautiful things

—A. P.

SLIP

6/14
HISTORY FINAL TOMORROW
STUDY W/ PHOEBE AT DINER 24
JUNIOR ART PORTFOLIO DUE FRIDAY
146
Greenware
Bisqueware
RING.
RING.
RING.
RING.

Hello?
It's me.
Phoebe! When are we meeting?
...

What's up?
Nothing. I just can't.
Why? Phoebe, what happened?

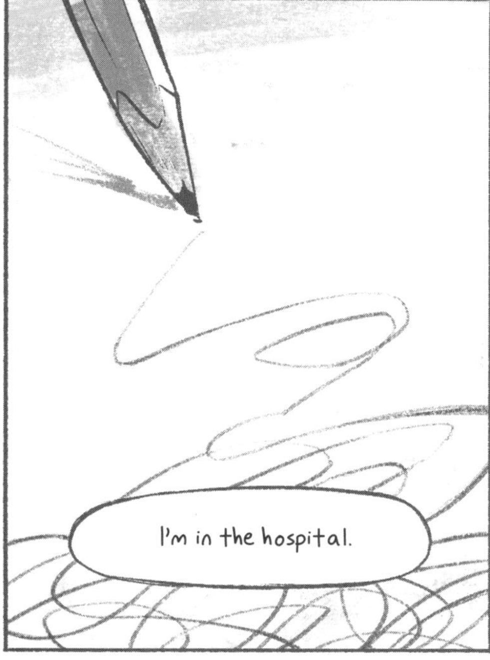
I'm in the hospital.

What—?
SNAP!

Here's my mom.
Phoebe, wait—

Hi, Jade.
Hi. What's wrong?
Phoebe's...ill. She'll be away for a couple of weeks.
Why?
She got... She hurt herself. She needs some time to get better, but she's going to be okay.

What happened?
Phoebe hurt herself. She's going to be okay.
How?
It wasn't an accident, Jade. Phoebe attempted suicide.

Jade?

Phoebe's going to be okay.

Jade, honey, put your mom on...

STUDENT RESIDEN
PACKING
clothes
shower stu
phoebe's address @ willow place
clay tools
toothbrush (don't forget!)
bath
clay
boxes
7/6

Are you ready?

I just need to grab my bag.

I can't believe you're leaving already!

I suppose it'll just prepare me for when you go to college.

hissss

If I get in. I have to actually create a portfolio at the Art Farm...

You got into the student residency intensive. Now just work with the goal in mind.
It's just Phoebe...
We're talking about you, not Phoebe.
She's my best friend.
I know. But there's nothing wrong with making more friends... or even having a little summer romance.
MOM!
Sorry, honey.
Just think of the artists you'll meet there!
I can't wait to see what you make. Are you excited? It's such a good opportunity.

Welcome to the Art Farm! I'm so glad you're joining us for an intensive.
BARN 2
Thank you.
We can get you settled in to your studio. All the student artists have studios in this barn, so there's always someone around to give you feedback.
ELECTRIC KILN
It's beautiful.
RED EARTHENWARE CLAY ×2
The view is lovely.
It is, isn't it? I always try to give this space to a ceramicist. In addition to the electric kiln...
CLAY TOOLS
It has the best view of our wood kiln.
A wood kiln? I've always wanted to fire one.

It only takes three days, and James, your mentor, was planning on firing it.
He'll occasionally include student work.

After an evaluation, we can discuss the *possibility* of firing your work in the wood kiln.

I'll let you settle in. The other students started arriving yesterday, so feel free to wander around and introduce yourself.

It was good to meet you. Jade, I'll see you at dinner!
I should get to work.

I guess that's my cue.

You'll call me if anything happens to Phoebe?
Phoebe's getting the help she needs. You need to enjoy yourself.

If something happens, promise—
I'll call.

Now *you* should focus on your artwork. I love you.
I know.

25 LBS RED EARTHENWARE
x2
WEDGING
SLAB
SLIP
COILS
PLASTIC RIB
Hello, Jade.

I'm James, your mentor for your residency.
Hi.
It's nice to meet you.

So you're working in clay, mostly animals, if I'm right?
Yes. I'm excited to be working in clay here. Linda mentioned the wood kiln....

It's why I always jump at the opportunity to work here when I'm not teaching.

While we can try to control the interior temperature and oxygen in that kiln, there will always be unpredictable results.

Wow.

They're just samples: rejects or cracked pieces.
They're still stunning.

They are beautiful. But I think that beauty comes from the unpredictability of the firing. We spend so much of our time controlling what a piece will look like...

But these artists have also proven their ability to relinquish control.
And it's that balance that's beautiful.

Linda said you might be firing the wood kiln.
Yes, I will. Sometimes I include student work....

But that will depend on your technique and what finishes are going to be best for the body of work you're creating.
Oh.

I'll schedule an additional evaluation before the firing and we'll see then whether or not you're ready.

Here's your orientation pack.
I know you got a digital copy, and reminders about our policies—including that this is a cell-phone-free campus—but this breaks down our schedule of critiques, our firing schedule for the electric kiln...

Student artists will endeavor to create a body of work or series of related pieces with a central concept or theme, the beginning of what could be a cohesive show. Technique as well as conceptual development will be considered by the admissions panel. Keep in mind that developmental materials (sketches, maquettes, writing, etc.) are an important part of this project and should be carefully archived.

...and the requirements for the work you're going to create this summer—

including the creation of a body of work or series with a cohesive theme.

Right now, your slabs are too thick.
Try to work thinner, but with braces and supports. You don't want your walls to crack.
Okay.

Well, it was nice to meet you, Jade. Please stop by my studio in Barn 1 if you have any questions.

I'm already doing everything wrong.

How am I going to manage
all this in just a month?
PLASTIC

You thought I could do it, Phoebe.
But then there was an "us."

I need a break.

What am
I going to do
for my series?

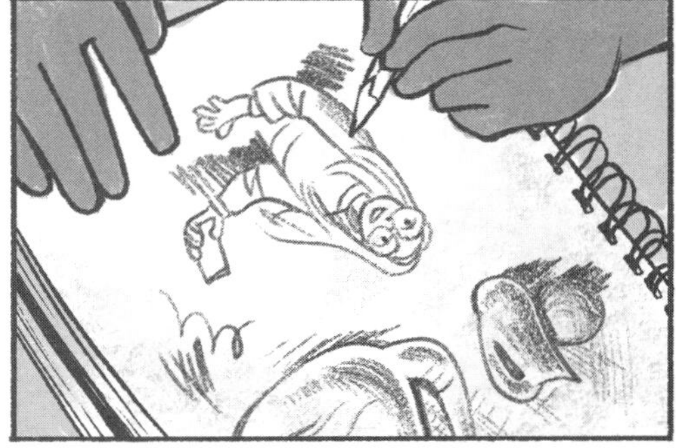

As if my shitty
doodles could
bring you here.

Diner
24

LOOK AT THIS! THEY HAVE A RESIDENCY PROGRAM WITH CERAMICS!

What the hell?

HOW'D YOU FIND THIS?
I WAS LOOKING AT SUMMER ARTS PROGRAMS. I SAW THIS AND GRABBED IT FOR YOU.

"DEVELOP A PORTFOLIO!" "BE CONSIDERED FOR ADMISSION AND SCHOLARSHIPS TO CITY ART ACADEMY!"
MY WORK ISN'T GOOD ENOUGH, PHOEBE.

YES, IT IS! AND YOU'VE ALWAYS TALKED ABOUT STUDYING ART IN THE CITY.
JUST TRY IT. YOU'LL GET IN.
You were right.
That's exactly how I remember it.

BUT WHAT ABOUT YOU?
DID YOU FIND THE PERFECT MUSIC PROGRAM?
I'M WORKING ON IT.
WE'LL FIND SOMETHING PERFECT.
I CAN'T JUST LEAVE YOU FOR A MONTH.
YOU'LL GO.
YOU NEED TO LEAVE ME.
You never said that.

What was that?
I'm hallucinating.
Or going crazy.
I suppose the only thing I can do is go work.
After all, it's why I'm here.

STUDENT GUIDELINES

Wow.

Do you like it?
It's beautiful.

Oh, good! I'm Mary, by the way.

I'm Jade.

Welcome! I'm guessing you do ceramics?

I try.
Well, you made it here, so that's a start.

So what's the Art Farm like?
Based on the walk I took yesterday, it's beautiful. There's an incredible sculpture at the top of the hill.

It sounds great.
Yeah. There's just so much—

uh...
Inspiration?
Possibility?

Possibility. I like that.

That's a good way to describe summer, too.

Full of endless possibilities.

7/7
Cock-a-doodle-doo!
7:15
It really is beautiful here.
The images yesterday must've just been stress.
Oh, Phoebe, what's happening to us?

Good morning.
Hi.

What are you reading?

Women Artists in the 20th Century. I'm really perusing it rather than reading. A little inspiration before I try to work.
And this morning's inspiration is...?

Flip it to a random page and see.

Today it's...

The Dinner Party.

Oh! Those are—
Yep.

It's Judy Chicago's celebration of famous women.
It's nice. I mean, it's kinda beautiful. I like—um...

It's...

It's so bold. She's not scared to say or—show anything.

That's why I like it. Chicago puts this huge installation in the viewer's space and demands attention. She asserts the importance of these women by making the viewer uncomfortable.

It's effective because it's uncomfortable.
Yeah. It makes me think that I need to push my work more. I just seem to be able to make nice things.

I think there's a place for that. Sometimes I just want a reason to smile. Your daisies certainly do that.

They do?
Yeah. They were a nice moment yesterday.
Thank you.

For what?
For what you said.
Oh. You're welcome.

Hi,
Mary.
Hi.
Asher, this is
Jade. Jade,
Asher.
Hi.

Does one of you
have time to give
me a crit?

I'm just at that
point where I need
some input.
Uh, sure.
Great.
Thanks.

I'll see you later!

Thanks for doing this. I'm just feeling stuck, and sometimes it helps me to have someone else look at my work.
Sure. I mean, it's why we all have studios together, right?
Yeah.
That one's mine.
ah!

It's really that shocking?
There's so much blood—I mean, red.
Red paint.
I thought it emphasized her arms and the knife.
Did Phoebe look like this?
There's too much. I can't focus...
I like that it causes such a strong reaction.
But if you think it's too much, I'll change it.
Think about anything else.
Don't think about blood. It's red. It's only a color.

Why'd you paint this?
It's Persephone?
There were pomegranates in the kitchen. That, and I've been reading Greek mythology.

Yes!
See, when Persephone eats the pomegranate seed, she effectively dies, right? Because it confines her to the realm of the dead. So in a way, she's committing suicide.

Suicide?!
Persephone is an analogy for the seasons.

Yes, but it's her actions that cause her and the earth to die every winter.

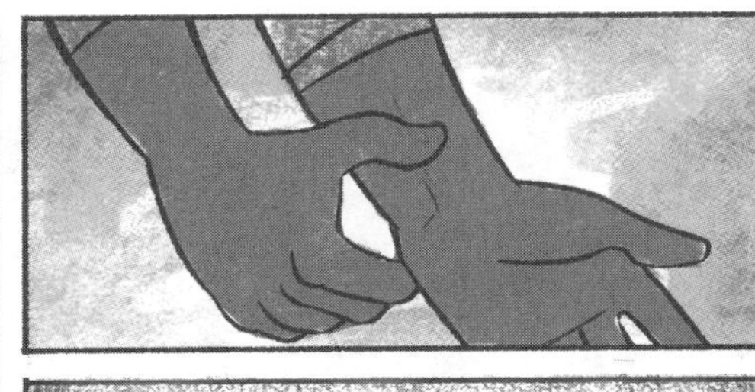

If I'd known, could I have stopped you?

I can't breathe.

Why?
Why what?
Why'd you choose this topic?

Because it's universal. Everyone struggles with thoughts of death.
But not everyone wants to die.
No. But everyone struggles with the fact that they will.

Some people talk about problems. Some people bottle them up. I paint them.
Some people try to cut them out.

Are you okay?

Uh...right. The point is that everyone struggles with the same issues. That's what makes them universal.
Why didn't you say them or write them or yell them out?

It's why a lot of artists deal with similar subjects.
Or did I not hear them?

So...what are you dealing with in your work?

I—I don't know.
I haven't had time to think about it.

Sometimes you can't see what you're dealing with when you're immersed in the work—it's too close to see.
That must be it.

I need to get back to my own work now.
Of course. See you later, Jade.

PINCH POT

HAND-BUILT HOLLOW FORM

-wedge
-build
-dry to leather hard (few hours
-carve details
-dry until bone dry (1-4 days)
-bisque (first firing)
-wood kiln
or glaze in electric
(second firing)

It won't be good enough.
And you're not here to tell me otherwise.

I need to have sketches or work in progress to present tomorrow morning.

How am I ever going to manage that?

That's awful.

Maybe if I make some maquettes instead...

NEEDLE TOOL

Okay.
But what do they mean?

Should they talk to each other?

That scale doesn't work at all.

Ugh.

Jade!
Hi!

Chips?
Thanks. What've you been up to?

Here. Take a look.
I wandered around for inspiration and made some sketches for tomorrow.
It's seriously beautiful here. My town is all strip malls and developments.

Is there actually a field of doors?!

I wish! No, I just drew them in.
It's sorta like Narnia.

Exactly! I carried *The Lion, the Witch and the Wardrobe* everywhere in fourth grade.
I actually tried walking through the back of every closet in the house after my mom read it to me.

Imagine how many wardrobes and closets have dutifully served their true purpose while disappointing children.

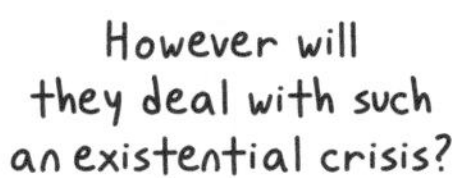
However will they deal with such an existential crisis?

HA HA HA HA HA HA HA HA HA

Mary, Jade, what do you think of the schedule?
What?

It's intimidating, but I suppose it makes sense....
It is a lot to accomplish in a month.

The schedule of crits and work we're supposed to do. What do you think about it?

I suppose art school will be like that, though.
Well, I have it all worked out.
Yeah.

Wow.
WEEKLY OBJECTIVE
That's intense.

But what happens if you change your mind, or the direction of your work changes after our crit?

I've been making sketches and statements for the past few months in preparation. I don't think that's going to happen.

Well, good luck to all of us!
We're going to need it.

So what are you working on?

Um, well, I explored a bit to try and figure out my next installation...
Oh!
So, you're the competition.

What?!
Competition?

We're all competing for acceptances and scholarships.
May as well put it out in the open.

...I hadn't thought of it like that. I mean, we're all working toward the same goals...
Yes, but not all of us will achieve them.

I should go to bed...
Need to prepare yourself for the crit tomorrow?
Something like that.

Home, sweet home.

Kim is so much more prepared than everyone else.

And everyone else is more prepared than me.

This is what I need right now.
You, here.

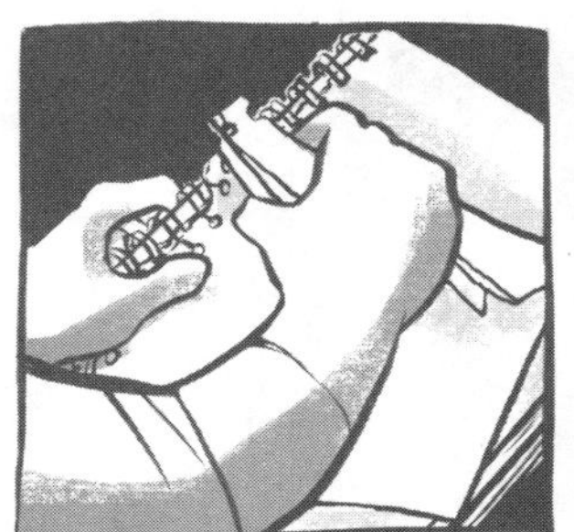

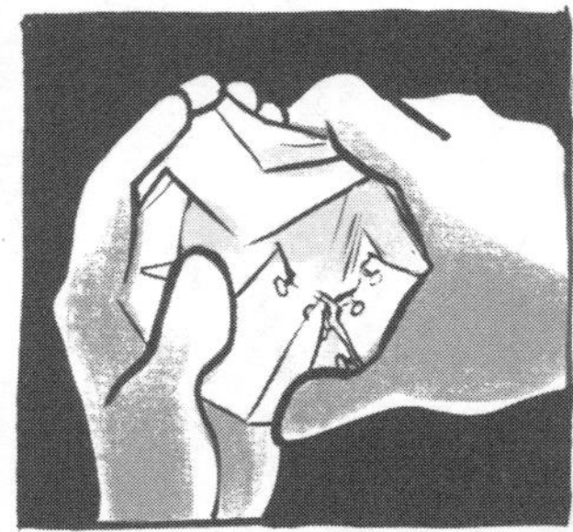

I wonder...

I NEVER DO WHAT I PLEASE
STUCK ON THIS TRACK
YOU CHOSE FOR ME
I DON'T WANT IT
DEE DEE DEE
I DON'T WANT IT

DO YOU THINK IT WORKS?

YES! IT'S AWESOME, PHOEBE. YOU'RE GOING TO BE BRILLIANT AT THE COFFEEHOUSE.

THANKS!

TAKE A LOOK.
TONIGHT
IT'S PERFECT.
YOU'RE THE BEST.

How am I doing this?

We're critiquing to help each artist push their work, to make it stronger.

Kim's work—
I'm exploring patterns in nature with a color sensibility that is contemporary.
As we can see in Asher's work, the driving concept is the connection between memento mori—a reminder of mortality—and Greek mythology.
Okay, but we want the viewer to see that, without you needing to tell us.
What do you think?
Conceptually, it's cohesive. But there are a lot of different media being used.
Which might be okay with a narrower focus...

Those are both good points. Considering the broader theme, narrowing down the medium would help to focus the work, making it a tight series.
Jade's work has the opposite problem.

While the work shares a medium and technique, it's lacking a concept.

Why are these animals important? What are they saying?

We don't know because the artist isn't telling us.

Maybe she doesn't know.

And that's why developmental work—research, sketches, and writing—is so important.

Keeping in mind what I've covered, take some time to push your ideas and focus your work.

Jade, if you could stay a moment?

These are beautifully rendered, Jade, but there's no concept behind them.
Why are you making them?

What is their purpose?

I tried to arrange them.
So they could have a sort of conversation.
But it didn't make sense.

And that's where the concept is important. What is their conversation about?

What does the fox feel that you're trying to show us?

Or maybe the fox is a vehicle.
In which case the question is—

what do you feel?

PHOEBE MARY FEAR
KNIFE SUICIDE
SMILING BLOOD
ANIMAL EYES CONFUSION
DAISIES PHOEBE
UNTALENTED TERRIBLE NOT
PURPOSE OVERWHELMED GOOD
MARY BODY OF WORK
PHOEBE
MARY
PHOEBE

Go to the library and find some images you're drawn to and analyze why you're drawn to them. Then find a way to give *your* work some purpose, okay?

NOD

That bad, huh?
He said there's no purpose behind my work.

That's rough.
I just don't know where to start...

Grab a book, any book.

You'll figure it out.
Thanks.

Jade?

PROTECTIVE GUARDIANS
ANIMAL EMOTIONS?
FEAR
HYBRIDITY
IDOLS

SIGHH...
I could use some real inspiration.

Want to go on an adventure?

Come on!
The hardware store?

-DING-A-LING-

Ooh!

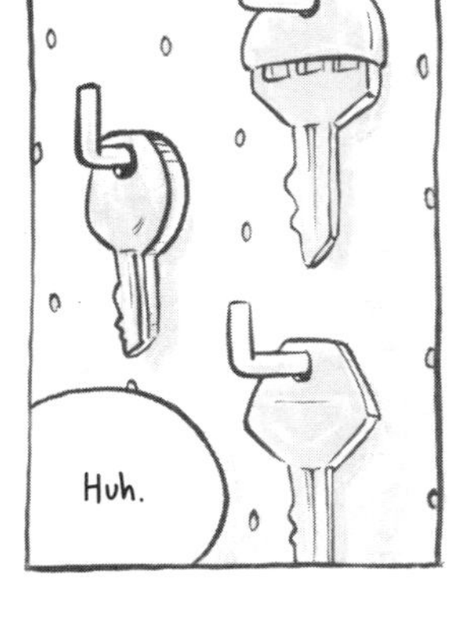
Huh.

I wonder...

Look at this.

Oh my god.
Jade!

The cheap version of Pantone heaven?
I worship at the altar of color.

Orange You Glad. Halloweeny. Pumpkin Butter. Really? What's next, Spray-Tan?
?

BLUSHING PINK
SWEET ROMANCE
SUMMER HAZE
KISS-ME PINK

What did you find?

That's quite the—
Let's go.
But—

AH!!

Artsy weirdos and your shenanigans!

What are you going to do with them?
Something. I've too many ideas right now...

"Artsy weirdos" was the best he could come up with?
At least I didn't drop the pretty colors!

It's amazing.
Almost like I can see the ideas racing through your head.

It makes me want to throw myself into my work, too.
I know you're thinking all the time but I can't see it.

I want to know what keeps flashing behind your eyes.

DONG
DONG
DONG

That's the dinner bell.

7/11

You!

You ruined it!
I worked so hard on that piece.

But I didn't do anything.

Your *ineptitude* killed one of *my* pieces!
I don't know what you're talking about!

God, I can't even believe they let you in.

Kim, I don't know what you're talking about!

Your crap exploded in the kiln and killed one of my best pieces.

I—
I'm sorry. I didn't know—

By the way, James wants a word.

Shit.

WHIRR
WHIRR
WHIRR
The kiln?
Kim said something about an explosion?!

Jade.
Yes, I unloaded the electric kiln this morning.
WHIRRRRR

One of your pieces must've had a bubble.

When it exploded, it took out one of Kim's pieces, too.

WHEN THE WATER HEATS UP AND EXPANDS, IT CAUSES AN EXPLOSION
Which means your building was sloppy.

You're going to need to wedge the clay longer and ensure your seams are scored, slipped, and sealed.
WEDGE
SLIP
SCORE
SEAL

While it's a shame your work is destroyed, the fact that it jeopardized everyone else's is the real problem.

This would be problematic in any course or studio.
I understand.

Your fired work is in your studio...
along with all the shards.
Okay.

Shit!

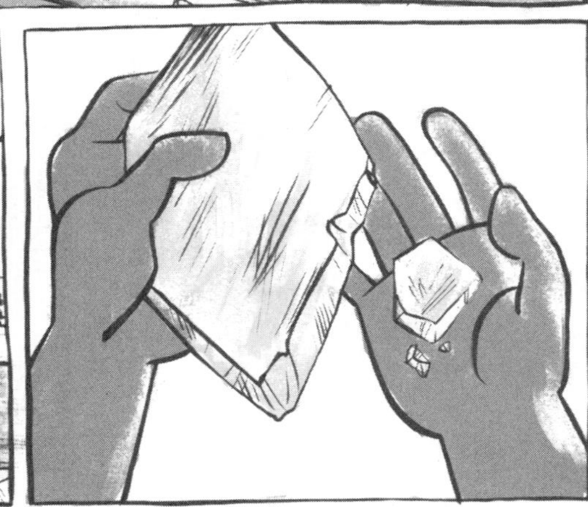

I'm messing everything up, Phoebe.

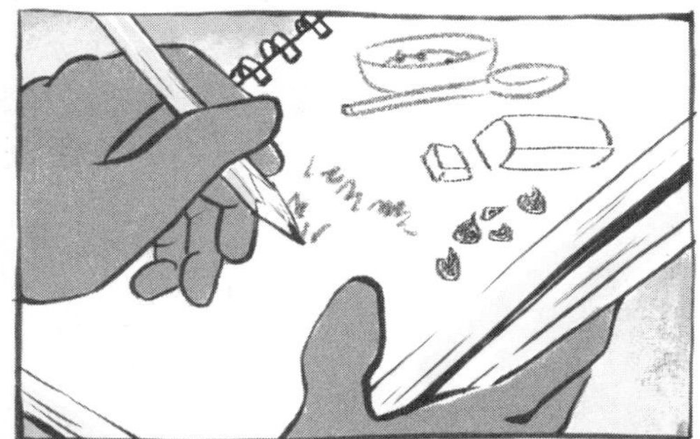

I THOUGHT THAT WHEN I WAS HERE I'D AT LEAST BE ABLE TO TALK TO YOU.
WHY DID WILLOW PLACE TAKE YOUR CELL PHONE?

Letters are useless.

I TRIED MAKING THIS WITHOUT YOU, BUT IT WASN'T THE SAME.
I THINK IT'S BECAUSE MISERY LOVES COMPANY, SO WE HAVE TO MAKE IT TOGETHER.
WE WENT THROUGH THAT LAST BATCH IN TWO DAYS.
MIDTERM PLAYLISTS CAN'T FIX EVERYTHING COOKIE DOUGH CAN.
PERFECT.
DIVINE.

That's exactly what I need.

Hey.
Hey.

Want some? It's cookie dough.

Thanks.
Sure.

I'd love to sit in the sun, but I've got to get back to the studio.

I should, too. I'll walk with you.
Great.

Is everything okay?
It's just a lot of pressure. The crits and everything.

I think they do that on purpose. Trial by fire and all that. Like, if you can survive this month, art school will be a breeze.
Really? Are you worried about it? You seem so confident.

You think so? When I was picking all those daisies, I enjoyed myself for the first ten minutes. And then I started thinking, I'm picking flowers. That isn't supposed to be work! Why aren't I working harder?

But it is your work.
It is! But I still felt like a fraud. Even when I got hot and my back started hurting.

So we're all in the same boat.

A boat that's rocking wildly around—

And approaching a waterfall—

And might be exciting—

Or utterly terrifying—

Or some strange mixture of both.

I can't make another piece that explodes.

7/12

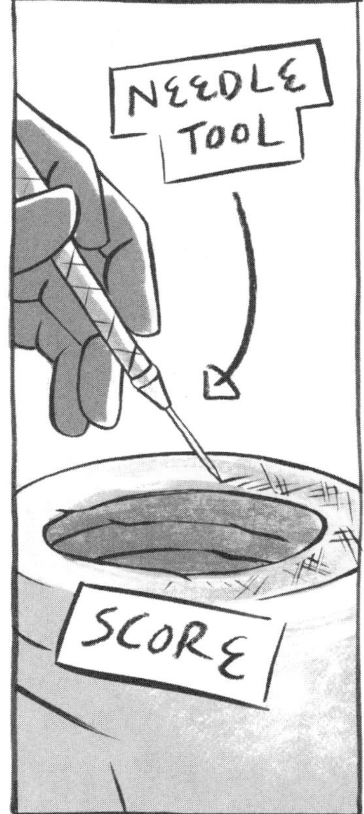
NEEDLE TOOL
SCORE

SLIP

SEALING

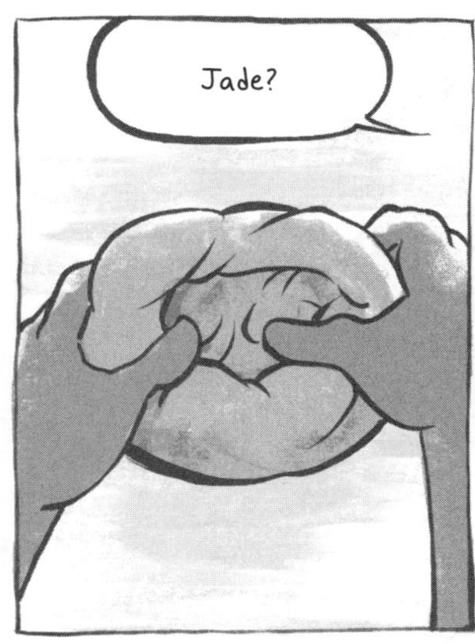
Jade?

Yes?
Hi.
Your mom just called the office.
She'd like you to call back as soon as you can.

Is something wrong?
She didn't say.

Phoebe.

Pick up. Pick up—
RING-RING-RING
Mom? What—
Take a deep breath, Jade.
What happened?
Phoebe's had another attempt.
What?! She— In the hospital?!
Phoebe was released two days ago, and last night she—
She was released and you didn't tell me? Mom—
Jade! Calm down. Phoebe's mother didn't tell me until this morning—when she told me Phoebe was back in the hospital.
I need to see her.
I know this is hard for you to hear, but she doesn't want to see anyone right now. She needs to focus on getting better and you need to focus on you.
Give her time. It's going to be okay.

You are not my Phoebe anymore.

Tell me what's wrong?
THUMP!

If I knew, I could help.

THWACK!

What was so bad about being home that made you try again?

Home's got to be better than a hospital...

Argh!

PROP
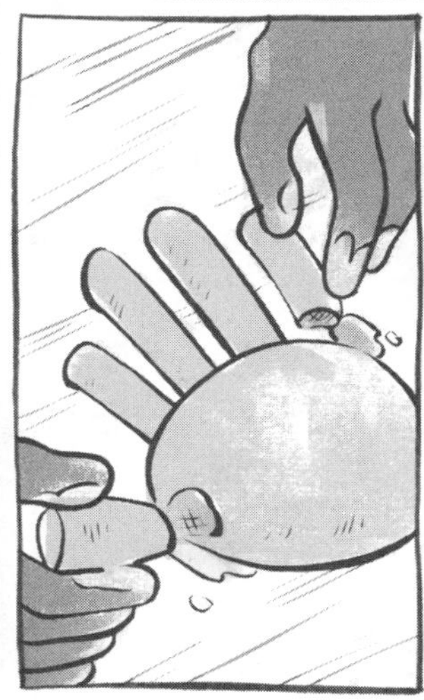
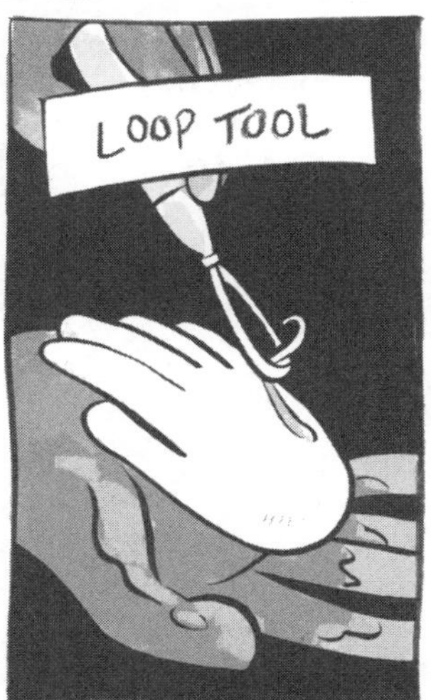
LOOP TOOL

DING!
DONG!
DING!

Yes, but are all brilliant artists mad?
No. Especially in the applied arts, where you have to deal with clients and deadlines.
You look like the studio!

Want some?
Yes, please.
Not to mention all the painters and sculptors who successfully kept patrons.

Which is kind of amazing considering what exposure to the chemicals in supplies can do to you.

Do you think madness can be beneficial?
To your story, yeah. People like the thrilling stories of madness.
True. So those are ones we remember and share.
Thanks.
Can we talk about something else?

I did read somewhere that mood disorders are more common among artists.
Are you mad? Am I?

Maybe because you can mine feelings more easily for your work if you feel more intensely.
There have to be some books on this.
You're locked away and I'm seeing things in fires.

There are a couple of boxes of donated books in the office. You could sort through them!

I need to stop thinking!

Uh, thanks.

I'll think about it.

Focus on the clay.

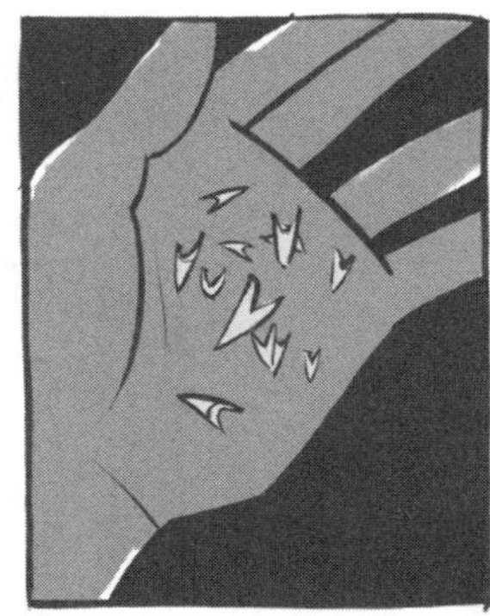

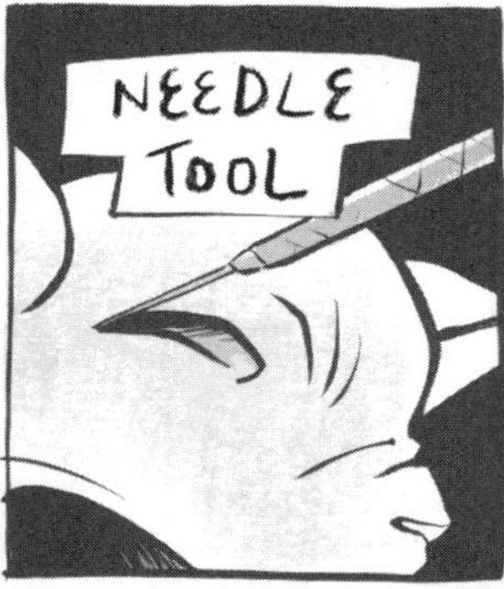
NEEDLE TOOL

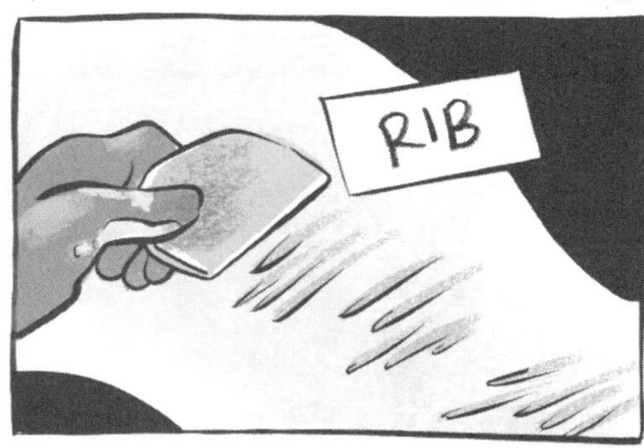
RIB

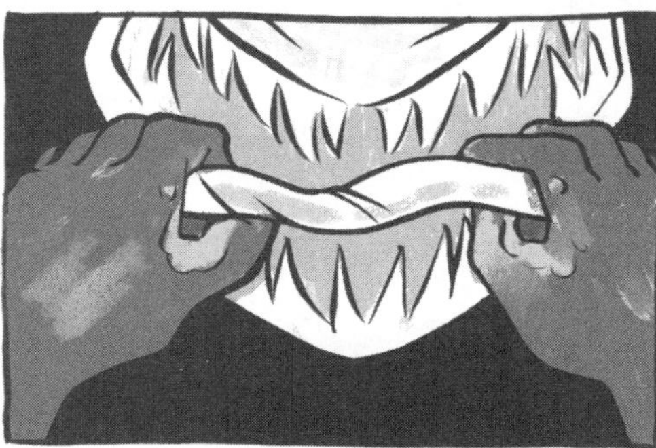

I have no idea if you're good or bad. But you're done.

If it isn't Sleeping Beauty!

It was a long night.
For a few hours, I didn't think about Phoebe.
LEATHER HARD

Productive, though.
Does she think about me?

Did you mean for it to be so angry?
I didn't mean for it to be anything. It just happened.

It is angry.
Like a good-luck cat that flings bad luck.
I've had enough bad luck.

Okay. Time for something nice.
Something nice?
Yes. You spent the entire night working.

Which means now you get to do whatever you want. And I would be a terrible person if I let you squander this beautiful day.

But— I don't even have a concept for my work yet!
What about that cat you just made?

What about it?
I think you may have something there. Animal and human with some serious emotion...
What were you thinking about?
I was trying not to think.
Well, whatever it was, it's...arresting.

And good enough to take a break with me.

You really think it's good?
Yeah.
Wow. Um, thanks.

Where are we going?
Have you eaten?
No, but even I draw the line at grass.

How about ice cream?
Ice cream would be perfect.

ALS

What are you working on?
A bunch of random sketches. I wish inspiration would just strike.

Add that to the list of wishes...
You keep an actual list?
No.
It'd be too depressing.

I wonder if writing it down would help, though...
Probably no more than throwing a penny.

That's it! I knew this was a good idea!

What is?
It's a surprise! You'll see!

You have ice cream...

Whatever. Inspiration has struck!

I'm an idiot.

Wait—

Did she like kissing me as much as I liked it? She hasn't said anything...

Stop mooning.
If I could just tell Phoebe...

Will this work?

THERE'S SOMETHING I NEED TO TELL YOU.

'KAY.

YOU KNOW I LOVE YOU, BUT I DON'T LIKE YOU.

ALL OF THIS SOUNDED BETTER IN MY HEAD.

IT'S OKAY, JADE. I LOVE YOU, TOO.
BUT YOU ARE SO NOT MY TYPE.
PHEW!

SO WHO ARE YOU CRUSHING ON?
NO ONE YET.
BUT YOU'LL BE THE FIRST TO KNOW.
GOOD!

THE FIRST TO KNOW
Only if she'd let me tell her.

Jade!

Hey. How are you?
Good.
I made something, thanks to you, and I want to show it to everyone.

Thanks to me?
Yeah, from our conversation about wishing.

I'm glad it was helpful! What did you make?
It's a surprise for everyone.

But I really wanted you to see it.

Come on!

They're special boats, for wishing. You have to write your wish and set it free.
My wishes don't come true. Phoebe's in a hospital. She's not my best friend anymore.

Come on. Make a wish. It doesn't have to be world peace.
I wish I'd noticed what was under the bracelets climbing up her arms.

Just a smallish wish.
A little bigger than a penny.

I wish I had answers.

I WISH PHOEBE WOULD START A CONVERSATION.

THUD.

7/15

WHIRR WHIRR WHIRR WHIRR

Ahh!

SPLAT!

I didn't mean to frighten you!
It's okay.
I find it's the best way to deal with shitty pieces.

It helps me get the frustration out so I can center the clay. If you throw when you're agitated, the pot won't be balanced.
Will you fire this?

I'll reclaim the clay and use it for something else. Transform it from a lopsided mess...

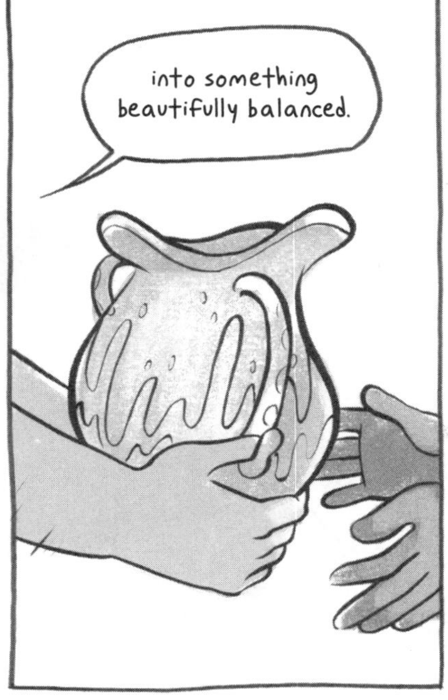
into something beautifully balanced.

It's so light.
Yes, but feel the evenness of the walls? That's what makes it strong. The one I just threw was lopsided. It would've cracked in a kiln.

By the way, I emptied the last kiln load this morning.

And?
Go to your studio and see.

I'll see you at the critique later.

BISQUEWARE

It survived!
Maybe I am improving...

AHH!

This can't be happening.

How did I do this? I didn't light you on fire.

But the kiln was fired...

Is that the same thing as setting a piece of paper on fire?

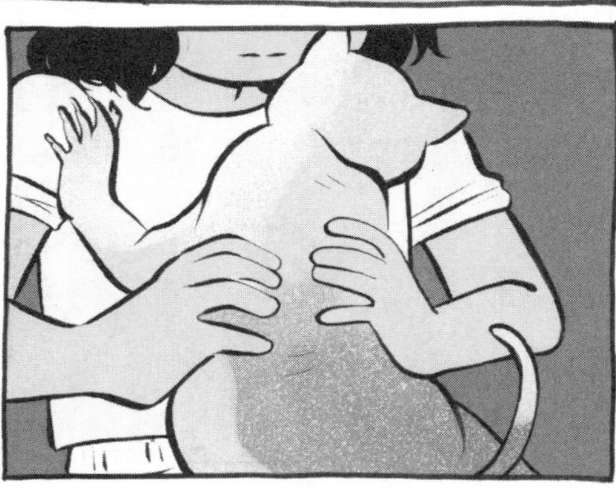

You're moving even though you've cooled.

YEOUCH!

What was that for?
And why didn't you break?

What are you doing?

No! I made you!

Damn it!

What have I done?

Where'd it go?

Someone else could be attacked! Mary—

Argh!

The drawings stop moving when the fire goes out.
But the kiln has stopped.

The cat could be anywhere.
Oh, hi!

What's wrong?
Nothing. Why would something be wrong?

Did you come from the studio?

Yeah. I thought I was going to be more productive.

You didn't see anything...weird on your way up?
Well...

Only if you count Kim trying to sing when she works. It's enough to kill anyone's creativity.
Where is it?

You seem to be in the studio a lot, though!
Yeah, but only drawings since that cat. I guess it's my way to avoid thinking—just keep my pencil moving.

I can't ever seem to stop thinking when I work. And I am morally incapable of the two a.m. bullshit.
What?
It's a great artistic tradition. Put some cigarette ash on a pedestal and say—

"It represents the ashes of an idea that was born, like a phoenix, from fire. The idea defies physicality, so only its waste can be shown."

...Or some crap like that.
A phoenix would be beautiful.
But would it flame? The cat is still clay....

Sounds like something Kim would say.
According to her, she was practically raised in studios and galleries.

Only two hours until the crit.

I need to go to the studio.

Perfect. But you have to make sure I go to the studio after.

I promise to drag you there.

What is happening with everything else in the kiln? Was it just my piece?

I've always been slightly suspicious of cows.
How can you be suspicious of cows?

How can I not?
Cows have really interesting bone structure.

Might be a good idea...
Ah! That's terrifying!

I'll make you a deal.
We go back to the studio now...

and I won't make this.
That's horrifying.
Not as horrifying as what could be at the studio.

We can go to the studio...
But you should make that, Jade.

Why?
Because it's terrifying. It's strange and unlike everything else you've made—except that cat.

So?
So maybe that's what your focus should be. If you figure out why or how you made that cat, it could be your concept.
ART FARM

Do you always know why you make something?
No. Sometimes...

Sometimes things just feel right.

I'll see you
at the crit
later.

Is Mary right?
Is this something?

But it's weird.
Unsettling.

What on earth
am I going to show
James?

PLACES THE CAT CREATURE COULD BE:

Ready for the crit?

The crit?
Yeah. It's in five minutes.

Damn it!

Is everything okay?
I've lost a piece. For the crit.

What happened? Did it crack or something?

I— I don't know.
...
I don't want to talk about it.

Okay.
Your work is so strong.

Thanks. I can't afford art school if I don't get a scholarship.
That's rough. Your work is really good, though. You have concept and technique down....
I can't seem to manage either.
You'll figure it out. That's why you're here— why we're all here. To push ourselves to make better work.

I can understand not hauling the cat over here, but no maquettes?
No. I—

I made some new sketches, though.
But I'm not sure... That is...

I'll take a look.

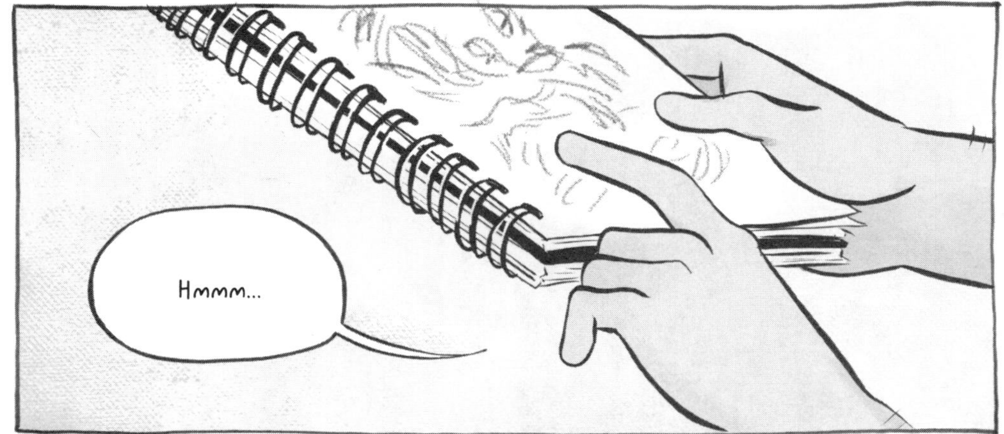
Hmmm...

You may have something here.

Which isn't to say that it's complete.
This is just the beginning—the idea still needs refining.

Why combine these particular animal components? What do the positions say about the characters?

There's a motivation missing.
But it's a start.

Let's see how it develops.

7/16

I may as well
try this.

WEDGED
CLAY

Remember to
make the slab thin.

I need a
break.

DEAR PHOEBE,
I LOST A PIECE YESTERDAY. I SHOULD PROBABLY BE WORKING RIGHT NOW TO MAKE UP FOR IT ~~BUT I'M WORRIED WHATEVER I MAKE WON'T BE AS GOOD AS WHAT I LOST~~. IT'S BEAUTIFUL OUTSIDE. DO YOU EVEN HAVE A WINDOW IN YOUR ROOM? I HOPE YOU DO. I WENT TO THE DAIRY WITH ~~ANOTHER~~ STUDENT ARTIST. ~~IT WAS~~ [illegible] ~~ENJOYED~~ DESPITE EVERYTHING ELSE THAT HAPPENED, I

Really enjoyed it?
Can I say that to you?

Really enjoyed what?

Going to the dairy.
Me too.

How are things?
Better than expected. But I've still a long way to go to get James's approval.

That sounds promising.
It's all thanks to your comments at the dairy!

Aw, I'm glad.
But I really meant, how are you?
Oh! Um—

Shit.

What is it?
A— It's— A—

A cat. It has some of my work.
It has your work?

What do you mean?
Jade?
Jade!

You stupid lump!

Why'd you have to interrupt Mary?!

What are you doing?!

That's not my art.

How do I
stop you?

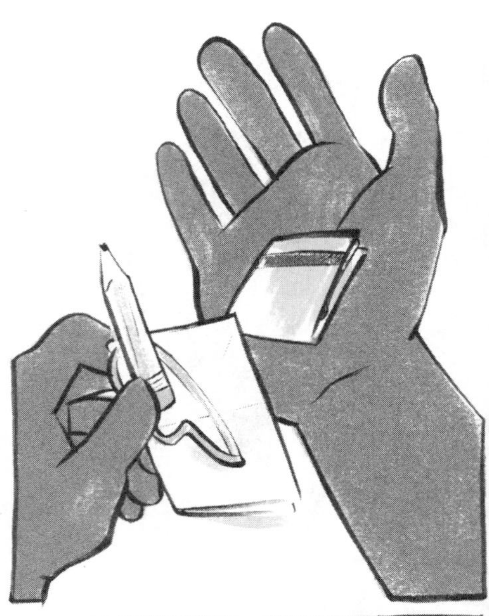

hssssss
fsh
t-t-ftt

IF I DON'T GET IN, I DON'T HAVE A CHANCE OF GOING TO ART SCHOOL.

WHAT WILL I DO THEN?

FINISH HIGH SCHOOL AND GET A JOB?

YOU ALWAYS WORRY YOU'RE NOT GOOD ENOUGH AND THEN YOU WORK HARDER THAN EVERYONE BECAUSE NO MATTER HOW YOU FEEL...
YOU DON'T KNOW HOW TO GIVE UP.
THUMP!

That's it?
All you needed was a comforting drawing?

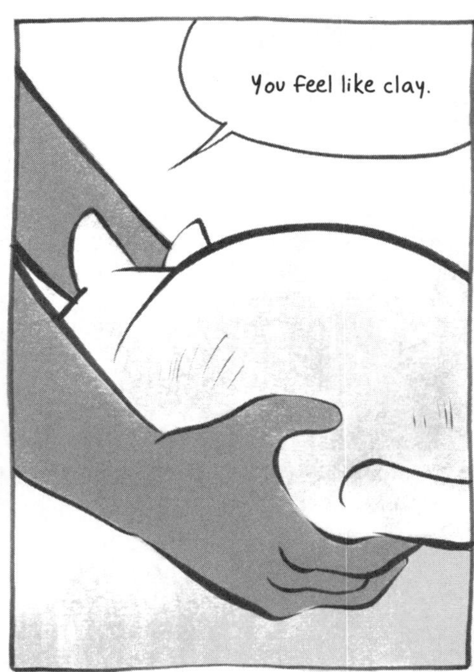
You feel like clay.

Not like something living.

I can't bring you back to the studio. How would I explain how you're in a different position?

I can't even trust my hands. I'm creating things I don't understand.

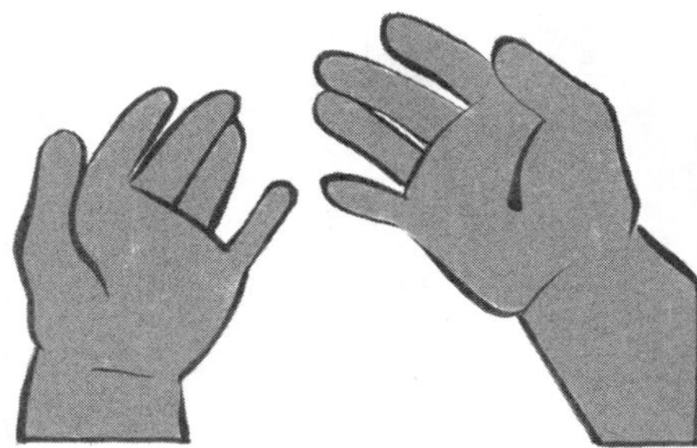

I suppose that's the thing about madness—what's real to you isn't real to everyone else.

What was real to Phoebe? Should I have seen it in her music?
CLONK

But everyone was writing angsty poetry. And that was her art.

Art's just a little piece of you, right? What you make.

Not who you are.

DEAR PHOEBE,

~~HOW ARE YOU?~~

I'M - I DON'T KNOW. AT TIMES I FEEL GREAT,
BUT I HAVE SO MUCH WORK TO DO.
IT'S NEVER ENOUGH.
I FEEL LIKE I'M WAY BEHIND EVERYONE ELSE, WHICH
MEANS THERE'S NO WAY I'LL GET INTO CITY ART
ACADEMY, LET ALONE GET ONE OF THE SCHOLARSHIPS.

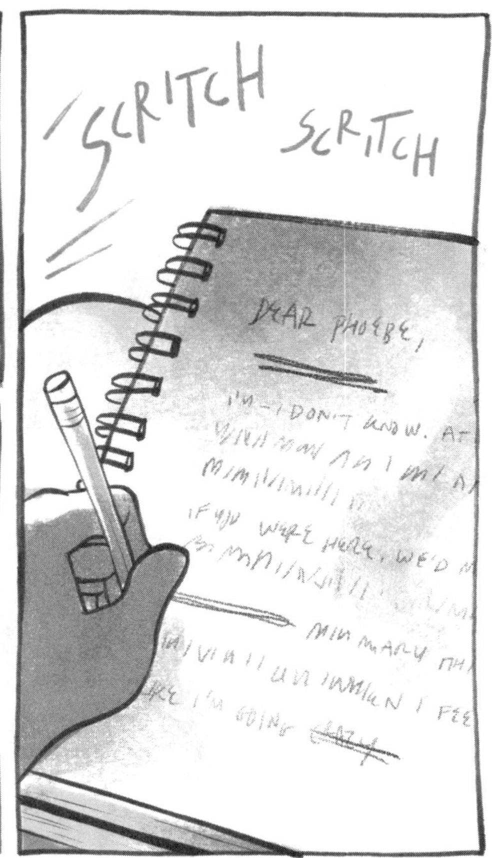

IF YOU WERE HERE, WE'D MAKE COOKIE DOUGH AND WATCH A MOVIE AND THEN EVERYTHING WOULD BE FINE AND I'D GO BACK TO WORK.

SORRY. IT'S NOT ALL BAD. I'VE BEEN HANGING OUT WITH ANOTHER STUDENT ARTIST, MARY. ~~I REALLY LIKE~~ ~~THERE ARE MOMENTS WHEN I~~ I GUESS THINGS ARE OKAY BUT THERE ARE ALSO TIMES WHEN I FEEL LIKE I'M GOING ~~CRAZY~~

AAAGH!

The drawing brought it down and froze it.
But only for a couple hours.

Argh.

KNOCK
KNOCK

What's wrong?

Oh!

A curtain rod? Is everything all right?
I heard something and there was this shadow—

It was probably just a cat.
But it looked bigger.
We're out in the country. It could have been something bigger.

I've run into dogs I thought were wolves walking back from the bathroom at night.
Or someone was pulling a prank.
It looked wolfish.

Ugh.
I probably look like an idiot.
Yeah. But a cute one.

7/17
MAJOLICA
RAKU
GLOSS GLAZE
MATTE GLAZE
WOOD FIRED
WOODEN RIB
WOODEN KNIFE
MAJOLICA
RAKU
GLOSS GLAZE
MATTE GLAZE
WOOD FIRED

YEOUCH!

Oof!
Is everything okay?

Ugh. I just scratched myself.
I'll be fine.

How do you scratch yourself while working? Misuse of a needle tool?

I said I was sorry about my piece exploding.
That doesn't make my piece come back.
No. But—
Hey, guys!
What happened to you?
Mary has this crazy battle thing set up.

Come on!

JADE ♥ PHOEBE
I've only been thinking about Mary and my work...

But Phoebe's still hurting, too.

Ready?

GO!

Ahh!
Stop it!
Yah!
Watch out!

Bombs away!
No!
Damn it!
Got-cha!

Oof!

Give me that!

Why did you take this?

yeeeeOuch!

I should just give up on you.

Move on to the next piece.

But why do you keep coming back to torture me?

rustle
snap
rustle
It's just a photo.
I could have let it go.

So this is where you disappeared to. You didn't want to stay for the color fight?
No.
I mean, I did want to stay—

But?
But I saw this in the bushes. It's from my studio.

Must be important...
Something from home.

What—
Are there any balloons left?
A few...

I think I can remedy that.
But—

It's not— You don't have a girlfriend back home?
No!

That's a friend.
I don't have a girlfriend back home.

Good.

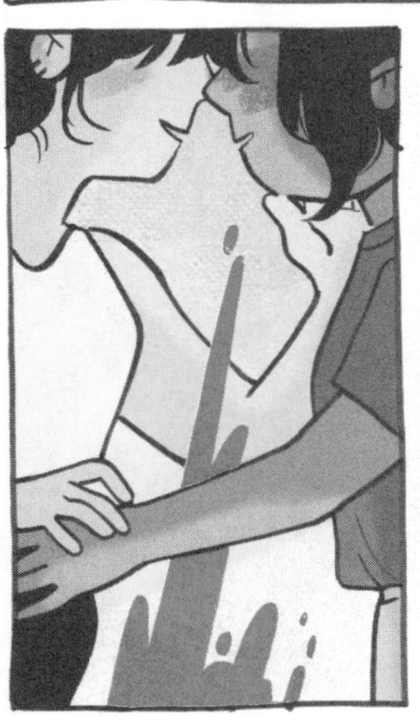

Ah!
Oh no!

Here.
We should probably pick them up anyway.
Thanks.

*Rainbow War, 1985

Help me with these, please.
I'm dropping the sheets.
Oh.
Who's the letter from?
Jade?

What do you think I should do with these?
Jade!
Are you listening to anything I'm saying?
What?
I was wondering what to do with the sheets.
I thought you wanted me to help you hang them.
I mean when they're dry.
Oh.
I could paint over them, or sew them. Could I make puppets?
I've never experimented with puppetry.
Have you?

What's up with you today?
Are the sheets done?
Yeah. I was just wondering—
I'm sorry. I've got to go.
Jade?

Here goes...

Give that back!
Stop attacking me!
Gimme the letter.
Now!

Damn it!

I should never have made you!

THUMP!
Gotcha!

Finally.

Dear Jade,

Your mom said you were at the Art Farm. I'm sure you're enjoying it. I'm doing well. I love summer weather, as you know.

Your friend,

Phoebe

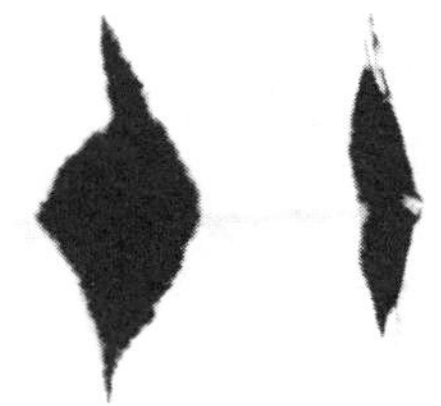

You can't do this to me!

Two lines.
Two typed lines.
THWACK!
A stick figure would show more emotion.
Why would you send that?
FETTLING KNIFE
Why did you hurt yourself?
Why didn't you tell me?

Was I a bad friend?

Did I do something wrong?

Did I need you too much?

But we needed each other.
Right?

What changed?

Jade?
Jade!

What is it?
You should go to bed.

What time is it?
Six thirty in the morning.

Ugh.
Thanks.

Sleep well!

Wow.

7/18

What's that?

Huh.
I wish I were as good as they want me to be

What are you doing here?
What?! Oh.

I needed some space.

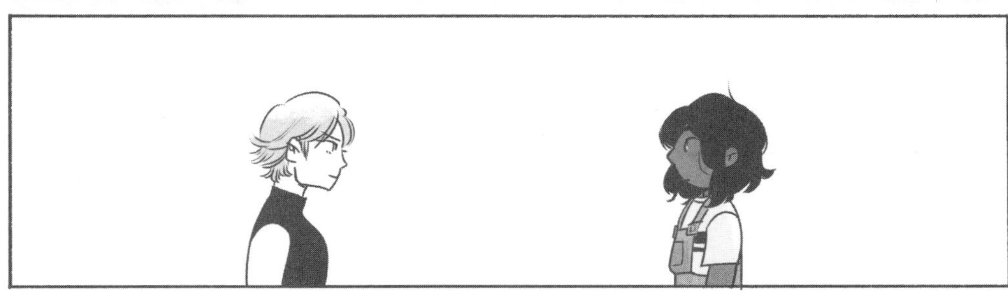

Um...

Want some cookies?

What's that?

One of the wishing boats from Mary's project.

Can I see?

Wishes are secret.
No one should read someone else's wish.

I don't know.
I mean, I wish I were as good as everyone wanted me to be, too.

It's not the same thing.
My mom is a curator and my dad's a gallerist.
Getting into City Art Academy isn't enough. My parents *expect* me to win one of the scholarships.

You wouldn't understand.

Just because my mom isn't in the art world,
and just because you think my work is terrible,
doesn't make my problems any less than yours.

Do you really think any of us want to fail?

You have no idea what anyone else is struggling with.

Cookie?

Um...sorry?
You just always seem to be in your work, or off talking with Mary, I figured...

You figured what? That I'd manage?
I guess.

Well, not everything is fine.
We're all under pressure.

I guess that's what happens when you throw a bunch of overachieving art-school wannabes together.

They should have a therapist on staff.

Uh, good luck with everything.

By the way—
because you'll find out anyway—
I just had a crit with James and Linda and I'm putting work in the wood kiln.

oh. Congrats.
Thanks.

Hey!
Finally
slept?
Yeah.
And ate.

All those things humans are supposed to do, but artists don't.
That's kinda sad.

It's supposed to be funny.
Oh.

I made that.
Yep.

It's really good, Jade.
You think so?
Yeah.

Kim just told me she's firing work in the wood kiln.
Are you?
James and Linda haven't said.
Why do you want to?
Have you seen the effects of a wood kiln? There's so much movement and life to it.
It's why I use earthenware clay. I think the color makes my work look more alive.
So the wood kiln would be one way of capturing that life.
Yeah. Make it intense. Vibrant. Those aren't the right words.
Volatile?
Yes! Like the emotions the creatures are feeling. It would heighten the animal emotions.
I should get back to work, but you should tell James and Linda that.
You think?
Definitely. See you later.
See you.
But no cat. Where is it?

Where've you been?
Why'd you disappear yesterday?

There was some stuff I had to do.
What was so important?

I don't want to talk about it.
First you didn't take part in the paint fight, then you ran away. I'm confused, Jade.

Me too.

You could tell me.
Phoebe's locked up, and I've been having fun with you.

I can't. Not now.
But—

Fine.

It's about the raging emotions that exist within all of us.

Emotions that cause us to act like animals.

Ah, so you've found the connection between the animal and human aspects.

Well, why don't you go ahead and bisque it in the electric kiln?

No wood kiln, then?

What do you think this piece would gain from being fired in a wood kiln?
Well...

There's an unpredictability to the wood kiln, I don't know what the finishes are going to look like.
And there's an unpredictability to emotions.
Sometimes you feel things and you don't know why.
Sometimes you act for a reason you don't know, because some animal part of you is taking over.

I think the finishes from the wood kiln will be like our emotions and the actions caused by emotions—
we can try to control them, but in the end there's always something unknown.

...
That's it.

Yes. You still need to bisque the wolf in the electric kiln, first.

We have a couple details to work out. You're going to need to do some prep work and an overnight shift with the kiln,

If only Phoebe—

I could tell Mary...

7/21

Nothing will move while Asher's here, right?

The cat's still missing.

Thanks for your help.
No problem.

We need to talk.

I—
Now.

Why are you avoiding me?

Jade, we need to talk
about the wood kiln.
Not now.

James and Kim are
already waiting.

CHIMNEY

We'll be firing for three days.

FIREBOX

DAMPER

STOKE HOLE

You found her. Great.

While we're firing, the kiln needs to be watched at all times. Temperatures need to be recorded, et cetera. Some local potters will also have work in the kiln, so they'll help out, but you'll both be required to do an overnight shift.

Both of us?
Yes, because you both have work in the kiln, you'll each do a shift.

Of course, I'll go over everything with you and check in frequently over the course of the night.

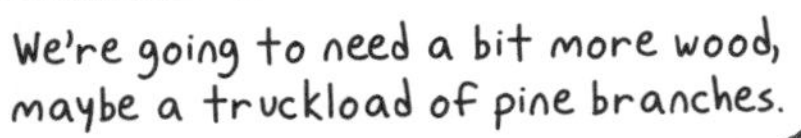

And I'll need to check on kiln shelves and see about raking out the ash.

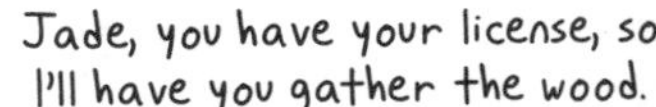

Okay.

Get what you can from the woods at the top of the hill. There should be a lot that's already stacked and just needs to be brought down.

Got it.

I♥NY

RUSS
SUSS
RUSS
SUSS
Who's there?
THUMP!
RUSS
SUSS
SUSS

YOU?!

What'd I do to deserve this?

I just want to help my friend.

I keep asking, and there's just silence. Or the lies I stuffed in your belly.

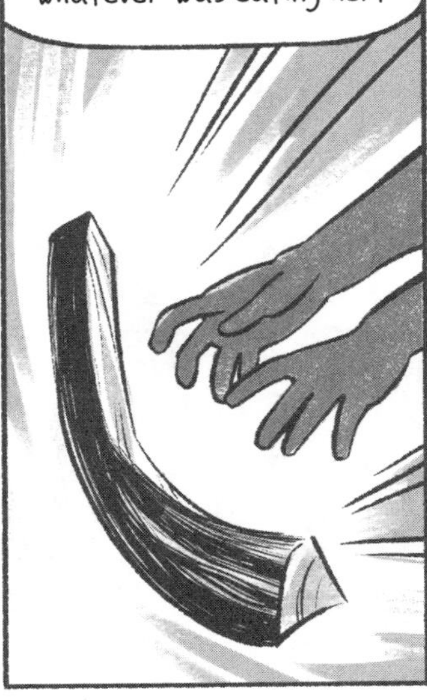
I just wanted to take away whatever was eating her!

I think it's gnawing at me, too.

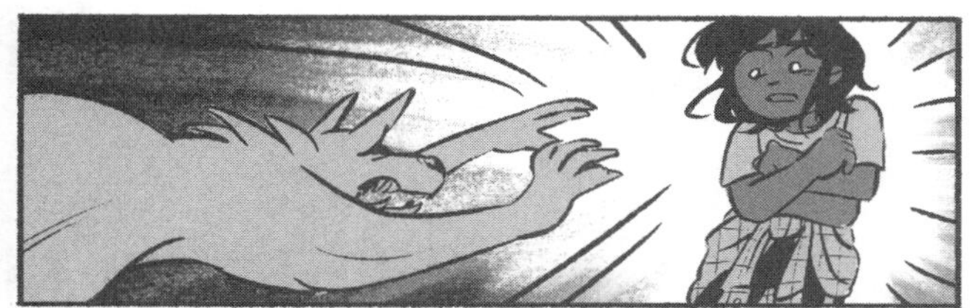

AHHHHH!

I'M GLAD YOU'RE IN MY CLASS.

ME TOO. LOOK AT ALL THE BIG KIDS.

WE'LL BE THAT BIG SOMEDAY.

IT'S TIME TO GET STARTED!

Maybe Asher is right...and Phoebe doesn't know why.

Damn it!

I'm asking the wrong questions.

How can you be you?

And me be me?

THERE'S SOMETHING TO BE FOUND.
SO I'VE BEEN SEARCHING.

IN AND OUT AND ALL AROUND.
UP AND DOWN, ABOUT I WEAVE.
UNTIL I DISCOVER-

IT'S TIME TO BE ME.
It worked.

The cat didn't hold for long. I have to deal with this now.

I don't have anything to tie it up with—

It'd probably escape anyway.

You have to let your best work go.

Shit.

I can make more.
Stronger, different work.

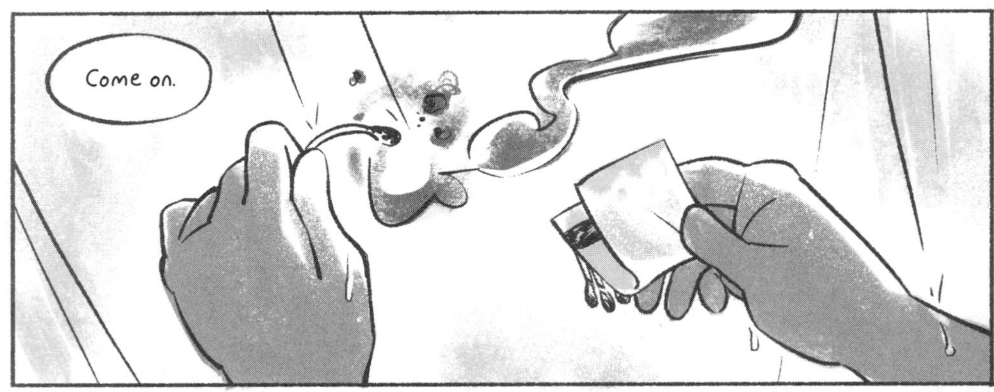
Come on.

Come on.

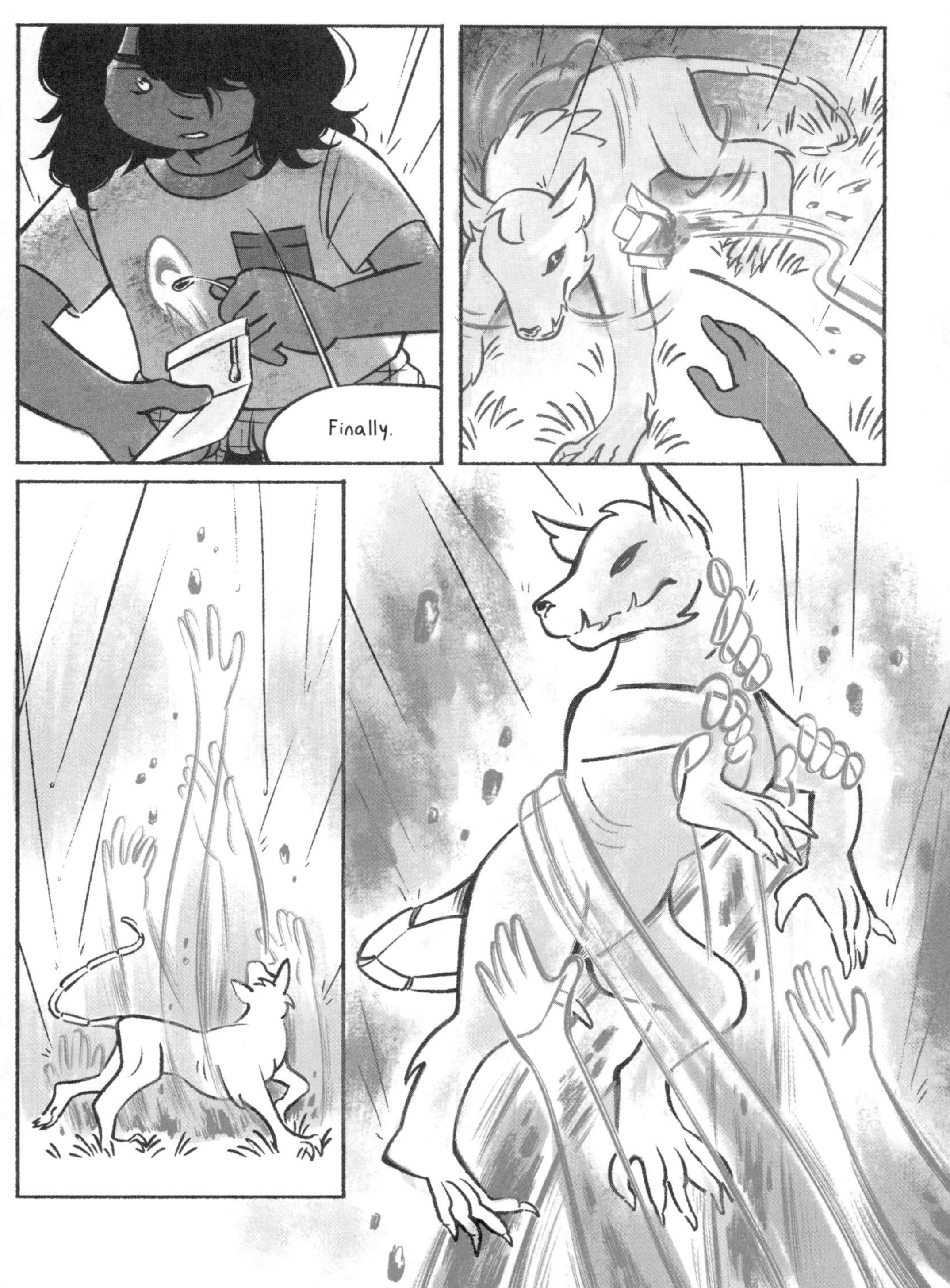
Finally.

CRACK!

I LET IT GO.

Ha!
BOOOM!
Shit!

What do I need?
I need to talk to Mary.

What the...
TAP
TAP
TAP
Jade?
BOOM!

Ohmygod.
Get in!

The storm's right above us. What are you doing out in it?
I was on the hill, getting wood for the kiln.

Okay.

I need to explain.
And apologize.

My best friend, Phoebe, tried to kill herself. She's been shutting me out since— since she attempted suicide.
That's who the letter was from.

I was frustrated and angry. And I needed time to figure out how I felt.
I started feeling bad that I was enjoying myself and she was struggling.

But I also know that Phoebe needs space.
And I can be there, but only when she's ready.

That's a lot.
Yeah.

So the past few days...
I was trying to figure out Phoebe. I was too wrapped up in it to see you or anything else.

I was really confused, Jade.

I'm sorry.

Basically, I need to be present in Phoebe's life, but give her space, too.
Let her know you're here, but without pressure.
Yeah.

How're you going to do that?
I don't know yet. A letter? A...token?
You're an artist.

Ha. Yeah. Probably a piece of art.

What do you need?

I need to stop defining myself by her friendship.

I'm sorry I couldn't tell you before.
I had to work things out first.

I— I really like you, Mary. And I really hope I haven't completely screwed things up.

That's good.
Yeah?

Yeah.

Though I think this apology might go better with a real kiss.

That I can manage.

7/24
What's this?

You know what you said about Phoebe needing a presence?
This is for her?

Yeah. Something that flies.
And rises from the ashes.

Yeah. It's not too dark, is it?
No. It works.

I have to take these down. Want to help?
Sure.

This is the last one.
CLICK! CLICK!
...documentation of process is so important.

I know. And everyone always seems to forget it.

It's ready.

Jade, do you want to do the honors?

Me?
Your work has really developed this session, and Linda and I both think you've earned it.
CLICK!

Go ahead and light it.

Woooo!
YEAH!
NICE!

I did it.

Hey.
Join us!
Thanks.
I went for a walk up on the hill this afternoon.
How was it?
You know that wolf you made? I found it in the woods—smashed!

Oh no!
I mean, who would bring it up there to break it?

I'm fine.

Jade—

But your piece! It was a good piece!

I have a whole wood kiln worth of work.

I like that one where it is. Besides, there'll be other pieces. Hopefully better ones, too.

That I don't doubt.
Thanks, Asher.

I'll see you guys later.
See you.

But how'd it break?
I mean, we can't have someone going around destroying other people's work!

I don't know how the wolf got there. But I broke the piece.

You broke it?!
I didn't really have a choice.

Does this have something to do with Phoebe?
Yeah. Sometimes you can't make a better piece until you break one. At least, that's what James says.

Right now, that feels true.

As long as you're sure it's for the best...
I am.

I'M HERE.
JUST SO
YOU KNOW.

Farewell.

You're beautiful.

Thanks, guys. Go get some rest.

It's time to get up, Sleeping Beauty.

I had an amazing dream.

What was it?
My wishing boats flew across the sky, carrying wishes.

I wish you could've seen it. It was beautiful.

I can picture it perfectly.

Acknowledgments

Once upon a time, a twenty-year-old art student spent a hot July living in a sixties van, building a kiln, and making weird ceramic creatures in a barn. Thank you to Salem Art Works for providing the inspiration for the Art Farm, and to my parents for supporting me so I could spend a month mucking about with clay.

Graduate school brought me two great relationships and this book would not exist without them. Autumn Guest, gifted writer and critique partner, thank you for reading endless versions of this book and ripping them to shreds because you saw their potential. Continual thanks to Jen Linnan, agent extraordinaire.

Querying this manuscript introduced me to two incredible editors. Rachel Stark, thank you for your early (and infectious) enthusiasm. Sharyn November, you are my bookish Baba Yaga.

Thank you to the Writers' Room of Boston, whose Ivan Gold Fiction Fellowship gave me a desk and a quiet place to work at a time when my bedroom was so small that I wrote standing with my laptop on top of my dresser.

Aatmaja, wonderful illustrator and friend, I cannot thank you enough.

Thank you to Elise Howard, Sarah Alpert, and the entire team at Algonquin Young Readers for shaping this manuscript and turning it into a book. Thank you to the booksellers, warehouse workers, and reps who got this book into the hands of readers.

And, most importantly, to you, the reader, because a book doesn't fully exist until it is read.

Marika McCoola

To my friend Marika, whom I admire so much as a person and whose work I loved long before drawing this book. It was a total honor to work with you on my first graphic novel project!

To Jen, my all-star agent and friend, I can never thank you enough for your care and kindness. To the team at Algonquin, thank you so much for your understanding, support, and dedication to making a beautiful book. Particularly Laura Williams—bird by bird. We did it!

To my mom, dad, brother, and late grandmother. I love you!

To my dear friends, for the phone calls, drinks, nights spent crashing on your couches, hugs physical and virtual. You all know my life changed pretty dramatically while working on this book and I really, truly wouldn't have gotten through everything without you. Particular thanks to Aliza and Hannah for stepping in as toners and making the book a thousand times more lovely than I could have achieved alone!

Finally, since this is a story about creative process and learning, I want to thank the excellent teachers in my life. Mrs. Atkinson, Mrs. Noll, Mrs. Kilgannon, Ms. Whelan, Nick B., Josh, Tom, Jillian—thank you, thank you, thank you. And hello to any of my students reading this!

Aatmaja Pandya

Mental Health Resources

National Alliance on Mental Illness

www.nami.org

National Suicide Prevention Lifeline

1-800-273-8255

The Trevor Project

www.thetrevorproject.org

Crisis Text Line

www.crisistextline.org

In a crisis, text HOME to 741741 to connect 24/7 with a trained crisis counselor.

Carter Hasegawa

Marika McCoola is an illustrator and educator and the *New York Times* bestselling author of *Baba Yaga's Assistant*. She studied illustration, art history, creative writing, and ceramics at the Maryland Institute College of Art in Baltimore and received her BFA in illustration in 2009.

Aatmaja Pandya is a cartoonist and illustrator born and raised in New York. She graduated from the School of Visual Arts in 2014 and has been illustrating professionally ever since. *Slip* is her first graphic novel.